Dear Parent:

Congratulations! Your child is taking the first steps on an exciting journey. The destination? Independent reading!

STEP INTO READING® will help your child get there. The program offers five steps to reading success. Each step includes fun stories and colorful art. There are also Step into Reading Sticker Books, Step into Reading Math Readers, Step into Reading Phonics Readers, Step into Reading Write-In Readers, and Step into Reading Phonics Boxed Sets—a complete literacy program with something to interest every child.

Learning to Read, Step by Step!

Ready to Read   Preschool–Kindergarten
• big type and easy words • rhyme and rhythm • picture clues
For children who know the alphabet and are eager to begin reading.

Reading with Help   Preschool–Grade 1
• basic vocabulary • short sentences • simple stories
For children who recognize familiar words and sound out new words with help.

Reading on Your Own   Grades 1–3
• engaging characters • easy-to-follow plots • popular topics
For children who are ready to read on their own.

Reading Paragraphs   Grades 2–3
• challenging vocabulary • short paragraphs • exciting stories
For newly independent readers who read simple sentences with confidence.

Ready for Chapters   Grades 2–4
• chapters • longer paragraphs • full-color art
For children who want to take the plunge into chapter books but still like colorful pictures.

STEP INTO READING® is designed to give every child a successful reading experience. The grade levels are only guides. Children can progress through the steps at their own speed, developing confidence in their reading, no matter what their grade.

Remember, a lifetime love of reading starts with a single step!

Copyright © 2011 Disney Enterprises, Inc. All rights reserved. Published in the United States by Random House Children's Books, a division of Random House, Inc., 1745 Broadway, New York, NY 10019, and in Canada by Random House of Canada Limited, Toronto, in conjunction with Disney Enterprises, Inc.

Step into Reading, Random House, and the Random House colophon are registered trademarks of Random House, Inc.

Visit us on the Web!
StepIntoReading.com
www.randomhouse.com/kids
Educators and librarians, for a variety of teaching tools, visit us at
www.randomhouse.com/teachers

ISBN: 978-0-7364-2746-3 (trade) — ISBN: 978-0-7364-8089-5 (lib. bdg.)

Printed in the United States of America   12

Disney
Tangled
A Horse and a Hero

By Daisy Alberto

Illustrated by Jean-Paul Orpiñas,
Elena Naggi, and Studio IBOIX

Random House 🏠 New York

Maximus was a
palace horse.

He was brave.

He was loyal.

He was strong.

Flynn was a thief.
He stole a crown
from the castle.
He put it
in a bag.

Maximus found Flynn!
Maximus pulled
on the bag.
Flynn pulled,
too.

Flynn got the bag.
Maximus chased him
onto a tree branch.
Maximus did not
give up.
But the branch broke!

Flynn ran away
from the horse.
He saw a tower.

The tower was a perfect
hiding place!
Flynn climbed
to the top.

Inside the tower,
Flynn met Rapunzel.
She had very long hair.

A woman named
Mother Gothel
kept Rapunzel
in the tower.

Flynn helped Rapunzel.
She wanted to see
the outside world.
She climbed down
from the tower.

Flynn took Rapunzel
to a pub.
She had fun.

Maximus followed Flynn into the pub!

Flynn and Rapunzel
tried to escape.

Flynn battled Maximus.

Flynn ran away.

Maximus found him.

He pulled Flynn
one way.
Rapunzel pulled Flynn
the other way.

Rapunzel asked Maximus
to let Flynn go.

Maximus liked Rapunzel.

He agreed.

He shook Flynn's hand.

Flynn shook
the horse's hoof.

Flynn took Rapunzel
to the kingdom.
It was big
and very pretty.
Rapunzel was happy.

That night,
the royal guards
found Flynn.

Flynn needed help!

Mother Gothel
took Rapunzel
to the tower.
Maximus went for help.

The guards took Flynn
to jail.
But his friends
helped him escape.

Then Maximus took
Flynn to Rapunzel.

Flynn climbed
to the top
of the tower.
Flynn and Maximus
saved Rapunzel!

Flynn and Maximus
took Rapunzel
to her family.

Flynn and Rapunzel
were happy.

Maximus was happy,
too.

He was brave.

He was loyal.

He was strong.

And he had new friends.